MW01109726

For
Brian, Beth and Liam.
Thank you, for all of the love and
support you have provided.

ISBN: 9781731204677
Imprint: Independently published

W. Thorpe Books

www.wthorpebooks.com

table of contents

Squishy and the Dark Shadow's Tower

Written and Illustrated by W. Thorpe

Goodnight

"Good night sweetie," Emily's mother said as she began to shut the door.

"Mom! Squishy's light… It is growing dim!" Emily cried out.

"Emily, you are old enough now. You shouldn't need a night light," Emily's mother replied.

"He isn't a night light. He's Squishy, and he protects me from the shadows. You know I am afraid of the dark," Emily said defiantly.

Sighing, Emily's mother said, "Ok sweetie, it would be good for you to get used to not having a night light every night. We can give his light a boost in the morning."

"Oh all right, mom. Goodnight," Emily
said sinking into her covers and squeezing
Squishy in close.

"Sweet dreams," Emily's mother said
as she turned the lights off and closed the
door.

Swiftly, Emily fell asleep.

The darkness grew increasingly deep.

Gently, Squishy's light went out.

Sinister creatures began to stir about.

Shadows crept through the night.

The air felt cold. The darkness blight.

With every nightmare, there is still hope.

When darkness comes, so must the light.

9

"It is so cold," Squishy shivered "Where…. are you, Emily?" Desperately, Squishy looked for Emily. Squishy crawled to the edge of the covers and saw a dark shadow slide beneath the bed.

"Is… is that you, Emily?" Asked Squishy from atop the bed. No response followed, so he built up his courage and leapt from the covers to the floor. What Squishy found was not his friend or a shadow. It was not toys and games, or what you would find under any other child's bed. What Squishy found is the thing that adventures are made of.

A blue ring was glowing and inside it was an image of a forest with mushroom trees. At the far edge of the forest under a sky that grew increasingly black, stood a dark tower that screamed, "stay back!"

Squishy knew the shadow had left him feeling deserted and knew that the shadow had taken Emily to this strange world.

Squishy knew what he must do to save his friend from this shadowy thing. Squishy stepped through the glowing blue ring.

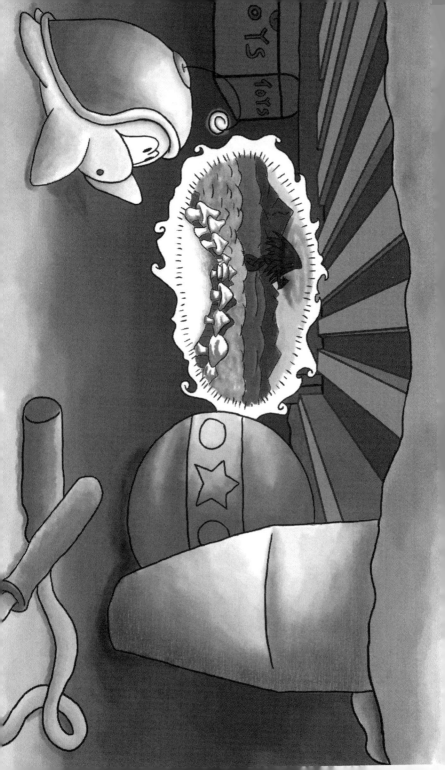

New Friends?

Blinded by a ferocious light.

Opening his eyes, he sees a beautiful

scene.

A wonderful dream that isn't quite right.

Creatures and colors like Squishy has

never seen.

But, the dark tower is not in sight.

"Emily!" Squishy yelled. There was no response only silence. With no ideas Squishy found a stump on which to sit. Squishy sat and thought and then started to cry. That's when he heard a sudden thump!

"Whoa there boy. What sort of creature are you?" asked a strange little mushroom man.

Frightened by the creature Squishy shakenly said, "I.. I am Squishy."

"Quit your stuttering boy. I won't bite. Now what kind of creature is a Squishy, and what are you doing here?" the mushroom man grumbled as he inspected the area around Squishy.

Squishy sensed he could trust this unusual talking mushroom. "I came through a glowing blue ring looking for my friend, Emily" said Squishy as he began to relax.

The mushroom man gave Squishy a puzzled look. "A blue ring ya say? Where's the blue ring now, and why did your friend come through in the first place?"

"It disappeared when I came through, and she was kidnapped by a dark shadow," replied Squishy.

The mushroom man jumped back in horror. "A DARK SHADOW! Oh, boy you are on your own. I ain't going near one of those!" He slowly started to back away and headed in the opposite direction.

"Please, I saw a dark tower I know that's where the shadow took her." Squishy fell towards the mushroom pleading.

The mushroom man stopped. "Ah yes, the Dark Shadow's Tower."

"Can you show me how to get there?" asked Squishy.

Seeing the sadness on Squishy's face, the mushroom man could not help himself. "All right, Squishy, The name's Boletes, but you can call me Bole." Walking back towards Squishy, Bole threw out his hand, "I will tell you how to find the Dark Shadow's Tower if you help me with something first."

Squishy jumped in the air with excitement. "Anything! I will help you do anything! Thank you so much."

Bole signaled for Squishy to follow him, and off into the forest they ran.

Through the Forest

Not sure who to trust.

Helping Bole is a must.

Nothing about this seems very real.

Hoping Bole keeps his deal.

Boletes had not said a word since the duo had left the clear opening. Squishy started to question himself about trusting this strange mushroom man. Squishy broke the silence and asked, "So where are we going? What am I supposed to help you with?"

"Sorry Squishy, I was in such a rush to help my friends I forgot to tell you what happened." Bole continued to run through the forest with little effort. "My mates and I were searching for a Vwulgre that has been attacking our village."

"What is a Vwulgre?" Squishy asked. He was panting, struggling to keep up with the nimble mushroom man.

Bole stopped. Squishy just about ran into him as Bole said, "I forget you're not from around here. Well, a Vwulgre is a type of ogre that draws its power from Dark Shadows. The one we are searching for carries a particularly large hammer. The hammer is made from the stump of an ancient tree."

"That.. that sounds frightening"
Squishy said as he shrank into his shell.

"It is," shuddered Bole's voice. "We were
caught off guard when we stepped into
one of the Vwulgre's well-hidden traps. I
barely managed to escape. I was searching
for help when I stumbled across you.
Now I need you to go with me to help my
friends."

"Right!" Squishy said forcing what little
courage he had into his words. Squishy
wanted to help, but was not sure how
much help he would be.

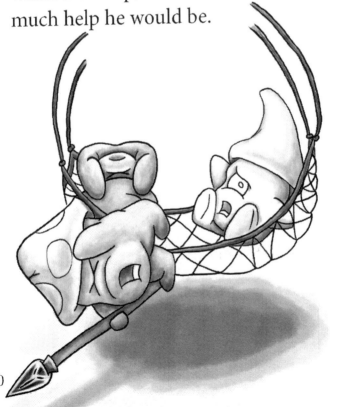

It was not until the sun was setting that they found the trap with two tiny mushroom-like men struggling to break free.

Upon seeing his friends, Bole exclaimed, "Boys! Glad to see you're still alive!"

"Boletes! You made it back! Did you find help?" asked a mushroom man with a bright blue cap.

"Aye, I did Porte!" replied Bole. "Squishy… time for you to work!"

"Uh, Ok," said Squishy nervously

Squishy looked up and saw Bole's friends where hanging in a net attached to the lowest branch of a large mushroom.

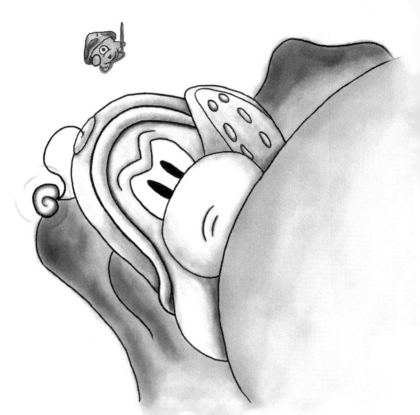

The mushroom looked like a tree. It had branches and roots but instead of leaves it had mushroom caps growing off the ends of the branches.

"You have to climb up there and untie that strange cord holding them in the net." Bole pointed in the direction of a large purple and yellow mushroom like tree. "You see, I cannot climb treeshrooms. I threw my spear at the rope. and it broke the tip of my spear clean off."

"All right, I'll try my best." Squishy was growing insecure with his abilities. "What if I can't do it?" he thought. Shaking, Squishy walked towards the large treeshroom, and using his tentacles he started to climb.

"That's who you brought?" grumbled the other mushroom man. This one had a blue cap as well, but it was a much darker shade of blue. "He's smaller than we are. What is he going to do?"

"He's all I could find. At least he can climb treeshrooms!" retorted Bole.

Squishy reached the branch the mushroom men were tied too. Carefully Squishy walked out on the branch with the dark rope tied to it. The rope glowed with a dark aura. A shadowy wisp radiated from it like a fire.

"What kind of rope is this?" asked Squishy. "It's like a solid shadow."

"How strange," Bole thought out loud. "Could it be the dark shadow's power is reaching this far into the forest? Hmmm," Bole said as he looked off into the forest. A grim look grew on his face.

"See, I told you that little runt wouldn't be able to help," mocked the dark blue capped mushroom.

"Hush, Bellos! I think this Squishy might just be the right creature for the job!" Bole shouted back excitedly. "Squishy, use that lighted orb attached to your head and place it near the rope."

"My lighted orb?" Squishy looked down at Bole. "Oh you mean my light! I use this to protect Emily from the shadows at night, but it went out. It doesn't work anymore. I can't use it. I'm sorry." Squishy sighed regrettably

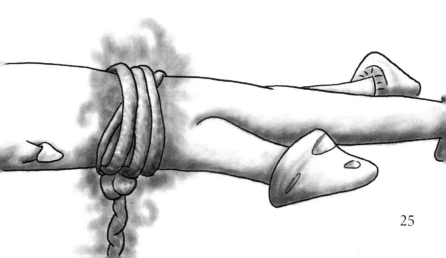

"Well, it seems to be working now, boy!" Bole shouted back to Squishy.

Squishy looked up and saw his light's glow had returned. Squishy moved his light closer to the shadowy rope. The rope began to burn, and wispy shadows dissolved into the air. The rope sizzled as more and more eerie smoke lifted into the air.

SNAP!

Rescued

The rope did sizzle.

And shadows fizzle.

With a snap.

Released the trap.

"You did it!" the mushroom men exclaimed.

"He did it. He actually did it. Incredible," Bellos whispered under his breath. "Thank you Squishy. We owe you our lives."

Making his way back down the treeshroom, Squishy replied, "No Problem. Glad I could help! Now Bole, about our agreement."

Bole looked down sadly. Hesitating, he said, "Yes, I remember, directions to the Dark Shadow's Tower."

"THE DARK SHADOW'S TOWER!" the other mushroom men exclaimed. Fear rattled their words.

Porte interjected, "he just saved us from certain death and now you're going to send him to his…"

"His friend was kidnapped. He's going there to save her. It is his choice." Bole interrupted Porte before he could finish his sentence. "Let's head back to the village. Squishy, you can make your way in the morning. It will be safer that way."

"That sounds good. Thank you." Squishy easily agreed fearing the darkness the forest presented.

Porte, Bellos, Bole and Squishy made their way back to the mushroom people's village. The village was small with many different buildings. Buildings were made from plants, twigs and other materials found from the surrounding mushroom forest. Music was coming from the center of the village, and Squishy could see a large fire.

Squishy and his new friends reached the center of the village and found the villagers celebrating the return of their mushroom kin.

"Haha!" Bole laughed. "One of our scouts must have seen us coming and told the village of our return!"

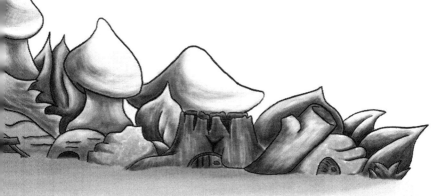

The village treated Squishy and his new friends to a meal fit for kings. Exhausted, Squishy left the celebration early and found a place to rest. Squishy didn't sleep a wink that night. Images of Emily and what might happen to her if he didn't make it in time filled his head. The moon sailed across the night sky and the sun rose once again. Squishy greeted the morning sun with great determination and prepared for the adventure ahead.

Squishy met with Bole and his friends at the edge of the treeshroom forest. Bole showed Squishy the path to the Dark Shadow's Tower.

"This is goodbye Squishy. We would go with you but we must continue our search for the Vwulgre," Bole said as he saluted Squishy. "It was an honor to meet you!"

"I understand," replied Squishy. He then said good bye to his new found friends and hiked off into the forest.

"You didn't tell him of the dangers that await him in the forest," Porte warned.

"We should follow him in case he runs into trouble. We may also find clues to the Vwulgres location," proposed Bellos.

"Yes, it is the least we can do," Bole said regret filling his voice.

Deep Grotto

Plants that smell with many colors.

This world is filled with many wonders.

Be careful not to lose your footing.

This world changes when you're not

looking.

Making his way through the forest Squishy noticed his path was beginning to fade. The forest grew thicker. Instead of an easy stroll along the path, Squishy found himself climbing over moss covered rocks and roots all the while avoiding stepping in swampy puddles. It wasn't all bad though. He could still see the sky shining through the treeshroom caps, and the sun was glowing brightly. It was still early in the day and Squishy could still see the dew drops on the grass and flowers that surrounded him. Wondrous smells began to fill the air.

"Where is that scent coming from? It's incredible!" Squishy thought to himself.

Looking around Squishy noticed the treeshrooms above him seemed to have changed species, and these new mushroom trees were releasing tiny yellow and blue spores. The spores fell like snowflakes twisting and twirling as the wind blew through the woods. The spores seemed to glow and light up everything around Squishy creating a magical atmosphere. Continuing to walk through what seemed to be an enchanted playground Squishy found himself gradually becoming sleepy. Everything

around him began to change. "Could this be because of the spores I am smelling?" Squishy thought. The landscape had completely changed. The treeshrooms appeared as normal trees and the grass began to look like sand. Worried, Squishy thought of Emily and pressed on ignoring the curious changes. Seeing a path ahead Squishy rushed towards it, and just as he leaped towards the path everything became clear. The path disappeared and in its place

nothing.

Squishy woke up to the sounds of tiny whispers.

"What is it?" the first voice asked

"I don't know. It looks weird" replied a second voice

"Shh, it is too late for it. Let's go before she learns we are here," the first voice whispered and shortly after the voices disappeared.

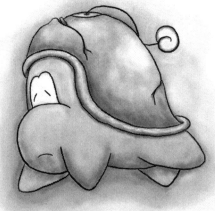

Pushing himself off the ground Squishy looked around and saw that he had fallen in to a pit of lush green grass. In the center, surrounded by a small pond, a glowing blue flower grew from the water. The reflection of the flower's light on the water brightened the pit. Squishy stood up to take a closer look.

"OUCH!" Squishy yelped.

Squishy had cracked his shell from the fall.

"If it wasn't for my shell, I could have died!" Squishy shuttered. "I need to find a way out of here and fast."

Building the strength to move, Squishy started looking for a way to escape. That's when he heard a fascinating voice.

"Why would you ever want to find a way out of here?" asked the soft, charming voice. "Don't you like the flower? You can have it if you'd like."

"I could have it?" Squishy asked questioningly.

"Yes, you can and you shall! Just take it" pressed the voice.

The thought tempted Squishy. The flower was beautiful but finding Emily

was much more important. "I appreciate the offer, but I must leave here to help my friend. I have no use for the flower."

The flower glowed brighter. "Oh? But do you know the flower can give you anything you desire! Wealth, fame whatever you want. You just have to touch it."

"I don't want any of those things. I just want to save my Emily." Squishy continued to search for a way out.

"Why won't you just touch it! Isn't it

beautiful?" The voice came again losing its charm and growing grim.

The flower's glow began to soften dimming the pit.

"If I was to fall in love with every beautiful thing, I would never reach my goals. Sometimes it is best to admire the beauty from afar, while focusing on what it is you truly desire, and for me that is to find Emily." Squishy stopped to see that the flower no longer glowed. The pit was now lit by only the sky. The flower moved, swaying back and forth transforming into something twisted, dark. This was no longer a peaceful grotto. A dark hulking creature stood at the center of the pond. Vines and petals encircled its body with thorns protruding from its blue-green skin.

"My flower is hungry, and you, will fuel its fire."

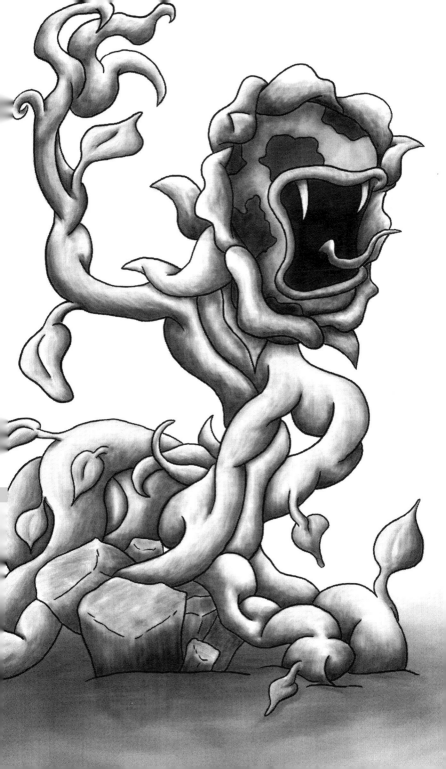

Fateful Battle

False beauty reveals the change.

What's underneath?

Something strange.

A creature wrapped in swampy sheath,

But something deeper lies beneath.

The swampy creature lunged at Squishy sweeping the floor with its vine like arm. Squishy yelped as the arm wrapped itself around him. "I have you now," the creature's voice rumbled. The arm slowly covered Squishy's body; darkness surrounded him, fear filled his heart. "I can feel the fear building inside you. How strange, afraid of the dark just like that little girl."

"Little girl?" Squishy thought "Emily!" The fear was expelled from his heart, and the small light attached to his shell flashed. The dark vines smothering Squishy began to glow. The murky tones covering the vines burst like a firework revealing bright green colors. The vine quickly unraveled dropping Squishy into the pool of water below him. The vines that had once surrounded Squishy started shrinking and forming into something more familiar, a human arm and hand.

Looking up Squishy could see the creature was in shock staring at her newly formed arm. "What did you do to my arm?" screeched the creature backing away.

"I don't know. My light, it just flashed." Just then it flashed again.

Shrieking, the once frightening creature cowered, "stop that." Her other vine like arm changed into a more human form. The shadowy colors exploded from its skin slowly shrinking until all that was left was a small human form.

Squishy cautiously approached the creature's new human form that was now lying still in the grass. The creature began to move, and Squishy dove behind a rock poking his head out so he could see. A young woman stood with long brown hair with two braids interlocking each other framing her face. A bright blue flower was laced into her hair that matched her beaded dress. Two wings then spread from her back as the woman stretched and spoke in a soft, yet commanding voice. "Where are you, my well-lit savior?"

"Is that a fairy?" Squishy thought as he hid himself not wanting to be seen. The fairy looked over her shoulder revealing her deep blue eyes. The fairy weightlessly lifted into the air and landed in a seated position on the rock Squishy had hid behind. Looking down she said, "there you are!"

Gifts

Courage will shine,

when true desire is defined.

Something that great, a gift divine,

buried deep for Squishy to find.

"Hello!" said the fairy. Squishy lay silent hidden in his shell. "I see your light silly, I know you are in that red shell. Why don't you come out?" Squishy poked his head out, and the fairy was hovering in front of him. "I'm Madri, Queen of the Fae. What is your name?"

"I am Squishy, but you were just a giant swamp monster. Why should I trust you?" Squishy replied, retreating back into his shell.

"Ah, well yes I was, but that was because the Dark Shadow's power had possessed me. That is what changed me into that terrible beast."

Poking his head out again, Squishy looked up "The Dark Shadow? He took my friend Emily. But how did…"

"He!?" Madri interrupted. "That thing, that Dark Shadow is not a he or a she. It can't even be described in such a manner. It is pure evil." Madri's face turned red with anger. "The Dark Shadow feeds on fear. That is how it took control of me."

Madri returned to her normal demeanor. She paused as if a thought had just made her very sad, then spoke. "Ever since the Dark Shadow took control of the temple at the center of the forest, my forest began to die. This is what I feared most. To lose that of which I love, my beloved kingdom."

Squishy moved to sit next to Madri. "That is terrible," said Squishy. "I wish I could help you."

The Fae Queen perked up "But there is! You, you were able to release me from the Dark Shadow's curse."

"With my light?" asked Squishy.

"No," returned Madri. "With your heart. Squishy, I believe you were able to push the fear from your heart with the love you felt for your friend. This feeling of love was then released through your light."

Madri lifted into the air and flew off. "I will be right back," she called.

Squishy sat and thought for a moment about everything the fairy had told him. He did not know how he used his light, or what he felt in those moments. He just knew he missed Emily and wanted to be back by her side.

Madri came back a few minutes later holding what looked like a glowing twig. As she approached, Squishy could see this wasn't a normal twig. There were complex designs carved into it with small vines and flowers wrapped around it. "This is my wand, and with it I wish to give you a gift for saving me from The Dark Shadow's power." Madri walked around Squishy looking him up and down. "It will be a dangerous road ahead and you will need protection." Squishy turned towards the fairy and began to speak until Madri cut him off "That's it! Your shell! I will imbue your shell with the strongest materials known to this forest."

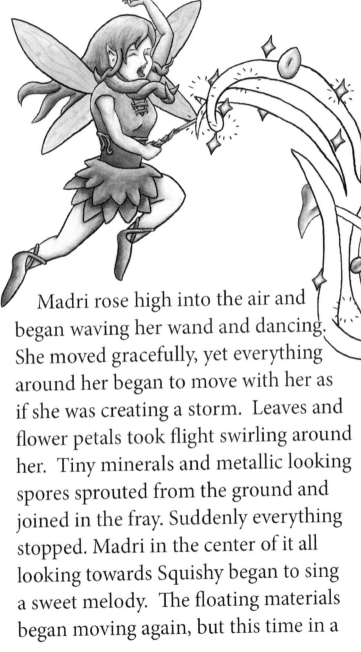

Madri rose high into the air and began waving her wand and dancing. She moved gracefully, yet everything around her began to move with her as if she was creating a storm. Leaves and flower petals took flight swirling around her. Tiny minerals and metallic looking spores sprouted from the ground and joined in the fray. Suddenly everything stopped. Madri in the center of it all looking towards Squishy began to sing a sweet melody. The floating materials began moving again, but this time in a

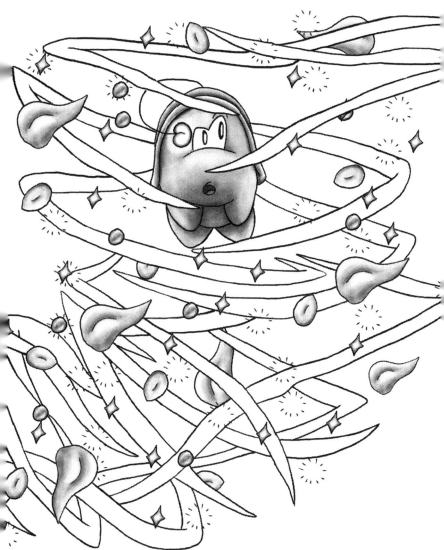

less chaotic fashion heading straight for Squishy. Squishy found himself amidst a small tornado slowly lifting him up. An array of colors swirled around him. His shell started to glow and change colors from purple to white to gold.

Moments later Squishy found himself on the ground again, and all was back to normal. Breathing heavily in the center of the grotto was Madri. She looked up and smiled, her face sagging from exhaustion. She stood up and flew slowly over towards Squishy. "Thank you again Squishy. Your shell is now indestructible. Should anything look to harm you, just hide in your shell and you will be safe."

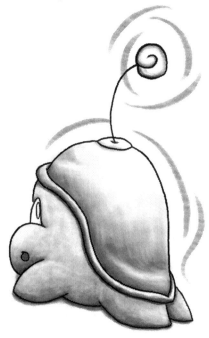

"Wow, indestructible?" Squishy said "That is amazing! Thank you. Madri."

"I am forever in your debt, Squishy! Now you must hurry to the Dark Tower and save Emily. Good bye, Squishy."

"Good bye. Will I see you again?" replied Squishy.

"I believe our paths will cross again someday," said Madri as she lifted Squishy up, flew him out of the pit and set him on the path to the Dark Tower.

The Vulgar Vwulgre

Mushroom forest growing colder.

Unseen dangers drawing closer.

The Shadow's presence growing bolder.

It seemed that hours had passed since Squishy had left Madri and her underground grotto. The forest had gone from bright reds and greens to muddy browns and purples. The forest once had

a fragrant aroma, but grew to smelling
of rot and waste. Squishy moved as fast
as he could to avoid contact with the
creatures of this decaying forest, but the
forest seemed to have no end. Wondering
how long he could keep this up, Squishy
just thought of Emily and pressed on.

Boom…. Boom…. Boom….
Squishy froze.
BOOM…. BOOM….. BOOM….

The forest floor shook. Spores showered down from the mushroom canopies. Squishy frantically looked for a place to hide. He noticed a small hollowed out treeshroom stump at the edge of the path with an opening just large enough for him to squeeze into and jumped inside

Just as Squishy hid, a slow, deep voice filled the area around him. "You far from home small stink."

Squishy peered outside his hiding hole
and saw what made the forest shake. It
stood nine feet tall. It's muscles stretched
its dark blue grey skin. In its hand the
monster carried a large hammer that
looked like it was made from a large
tree stump it had ripped out of the

61

ground. Squishy
remembered
something Bole
had said about
a creature that
carries a hammer
that was made
from a large
tree stump.
"The Vwulgre!"
Squishy
trembled at the
thought. This
is the monster Bole and his friends were
searching for. The Vwulgre began looking
under rocks and sniffing them trying to
find the "small stink".

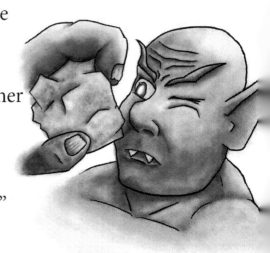

The Vwulgre grumbled, "Somewhere
close small stink sits. I want taste what
stench doesn't fits!"

Squishy hid inside his shell and didn't
move a muscle. He could hear the
monster stepping closer.

CRUNCH

Squishy's stump crumbled underneath the Vwulgres massive wooden hammer.

"HWUH HWUH HWUHHH look like I accidentally crush small stink!" laughed the Vwulgre.

The monster lifted its hammer.

"WHUA?" the Vwulgre stepped back in confusion.

On the ground where the hammer had fallen, laid Squishy perfectly unharmed hidden in his shell. Squishy popped out his arms and looked up at the giant beast. The giant creature looked at his hammer and noticed that Squishy had left a large dent in the massive hammer.

"YOU DENT HAMMER! I SMASH WITH 'SLAMMER!" Yelling with rage, the monster lifted its hammer once more.
SLAM SLAM SLAM

The Vwulgre hit Squishy with its hammer over and over again. Piece by piece the hammer grew smaller as wooden chips broke off of it.

SLAM SLAM SLAM

SLAM SLam slam

slam slam TINK!

The hammer was now nothing more than a stick. The magic Madri used had given Squishy's shell the strength to fend off the Vwulgre's mighty hammer.

"MY SLAMMER! YOU SMALL STINK BROKE MY SLAMMER!" the Vwulgre stepped back in fear. "But how... how did slammer break? I make with mighty ancient tree?" Without its hammer the Vwulgre felt weak and vulnerable.

Feigning confidence, the Vwulgre grumbled, "Hwuh no worries I still eat small stink!" The Vwulgre stepped forward slowly. It was still unsure of what Squishy was capable of. Squishy just destroyed his ancient hammer with little effort.

The ogre-like creature's massive hand reached down and grabbed Squishy. Squishy struggled to break free but was unable to escape the monster's grasp.

"Hwuh whuh whuh small stink have hard shell is all. No problem. I just suck you right out like shellfish," The beast said as it opened its mouth wide.

Three large sticks struck the Vwulgre's head. The ogre fell to the ground, and Squishy was thrown free.

The beast was knocked out, and on top of it stood a small mushroom man holding a broken spear.

"BOLE, PORTE, BELLOS, you saved me! I thought you all said you wouldn't come this way."

"Oi, Boyo we did, but we couldn't bare the thought of letting a little one like you go in the forest alone." Bole stepped off the hulking creature and walked towards Squishy. "We had just caught up when we saw that Vwulgre smashing away with his slammer." Porte and Bellos began tying up Vwulgre.

Squishy sighed with relief, "I cannot believe I was almost eaten by that, thanks friends!"

"Don't thank us," Porte said finishing up his last knot. "If it wasn't for your shell breaking its hammer, we wouldn't have been able to help you."

Bellos interrupted Porte, "Without its hammer, the Vwulgre is easy to take down. Vwulgres become fearful when they lose their hammers. Making them vulnerable"

"Porte… Bellos, take that Vwulgre back to the village," directed Bole. "Judging by the trap Porte and Bellos were caught in earlier. This Vwulgre knows something about the other evil creatures that have begun to plague our world. I will escort Squishy the rest of the way to the Dark Shadow's Tower."

Bellos and Porte carried the Vwulgre in the direction of the village. Reaching out a hand to Squishy, Bole helped Squishy off the ground and they continued on the path to the Dark Shadow's Tower.

The Dark Tower Draws Near

Trials lie ahead

Dangerous grounds Squishy will tread.

Puzzles Squishy must decipher

Or else fall to the shadows fire.

"There it is, the Dark Shadow's Tower." Bole said.

The dark tower stood on a small piece of land supported by a bridge. It was surrounded by a large crater as if the tower had collided with the earth long ago. Along the sides of the bridge stood six giant stone statues with glowing eyes that lit up the bridge. The tower itself looked like a willow tree that had frozen in time and grown black from the lack of life surrounding it.

"It's much scarier than when I saw it before," Squishy said.

"Yes, Squishy. This is why most creatures don't come this close. The tower looks as if it will suck the life straight out of you." Bole said grimly "Now this is where I leave you. "

"You're leaving!?" questioned Squishy.

"I need to get back to my village and help with the Vwulgre." Bole began to step in the direction of his home and then stopped. "One more thing, I just remembered I found this map on the Vwulgre. I believe it's a map of the tower." Bole pulled out a map from his pack and opened it up.

Squishy looked at the map then rolled it up and put it in a safe spot. "I don't know how I'll ever repay you, Bole."

Bole bowed to Squishy, "All I ask is that you save your friend and get out alive! When you get out, I'll meet you in the clearing where we first met."

And with that Bole, the mushroom warrior, jumped off into the forest.

75

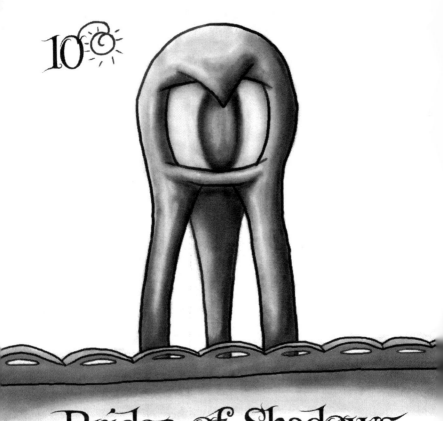

Bridge of Shadows

Giant statues light the way.

Passerby's led astray.

Revealed to Squishy a paper guide.

By which he must now abide.

Squishy arrived at the bridge and looked up at the giant stone statues. These were unlike any statues Squishy had seen. They seemed to be alive. The eyes of each statue lit up large areas along the bridge like a spotlight. Squishy started to cross but stopped as he saw a bird fly overhead through the giant statues gaze. The floor of the bridge disappeared where the bird had made a shadow.

Squishy then threw a rock onto the bridge, and it fell straight through into the crater's abyss. Squishy remembered his map and opened it up. The map had different clues to different sections of the tower. Next to the bridge it read:

In the light, all is clear. In the shadow, all will disappear.

Squishy thought to himself, "How will I ever get across? No matter what I do, I will make a shadow when I step into those giant statue's gazes."

"Light" Squishy jumped at the whisper.

"What was that?" Thought Squishy.

"Light, use the light" the whisper sounded again.

Squishy looked around "It sounds like Emily. How can it be?"

"Use your light Squishy!" the whisper sounded just a bit louder this time.

"My light? Yes, my light!" Squishy

said excitedly remembering his light was working in this strange world.

Squishy began to think again about what the whisper had said to him. He thought about the clue from the map and how it might relate to what the whisper said. "How do I use my light to cross this bridge?" thought Squishy as he walked closer to the bridge. He raised his right tentacle to create a shadow in the first statue's gaze. The bridge disappeared. Squishy then shined his light on his

tentacles shadow. The bridge reappeared.

Squishy jumped excitedly. He had a brilliant idea. Because of Squishy's excitement his light began to glow even more. Squishy extended his light as long as he could. He used his tentacles to stand on top of the light.

Squishy then began to hop across the bridge on his light.

Squishy hopped all the way across the bridge with no problems at all. On the other side, Squishy stared up at the Dark Shadow's Tower and saw how large it truly was. The tower was as black as night and a dark aura radiated from its tangled shape. Squishy feared what he would find inside.

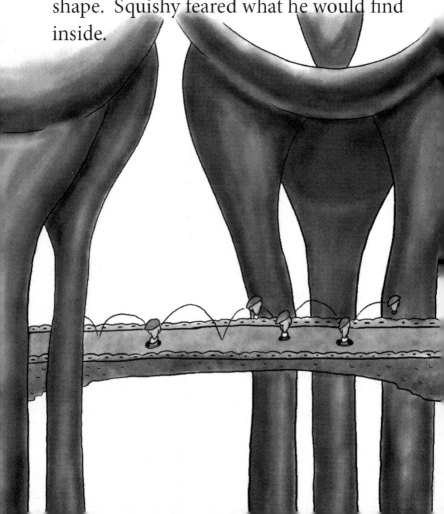

The Dark Shadow's Tower

Shadows overwhelmed.

Go away, turn back,

Dark voices compelled.

Expelling the black,

Squishy's light shined bright.

Squishy made his way through the winding halls of the dark tower. His light lit the way forcing back the shadows. Squishy came across a large wooden door. The door creaked and cracked as Squishy

82

slowly opened it. Wooden chips broke off and crumbled to the floor, and Squishy began to hear the sounds of chirping.

The room was large and glowed with

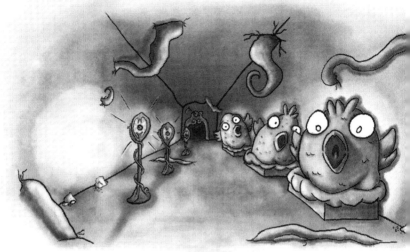

light from three light posts spread out across the floor. In front of each light sat a large baby bird in a nest. The birds were chirping loudly when Squishy entered the room. Each bird turned at the same time to look at the noise Squishy made. At the sight of Squishy the baby birds began chirping and squirming more wildly. There was only one path between the lights and the birds, and the birds were hungry.

"This must be one of the traps," Squishy thought. "I better check out the map."

Squishy looked at his map and found a picture of a light drawn next to a bird in a nest. It read:

In the light alert in nest, in its absence take a rest.

"I don't get riddles!" Squishy exclaimed and threw a rock across the room in his frustration.

The rock flew in front of the first bird, and the bird suddenly stopped chirping and began to breathe in air. The bird's head scrunched up into its body as a huge gust of wind began to enter the bird's mouth. The rock was sucked up and eaten within seconds by the baby bird. It then returned to its chirping and began flailing even more violently.

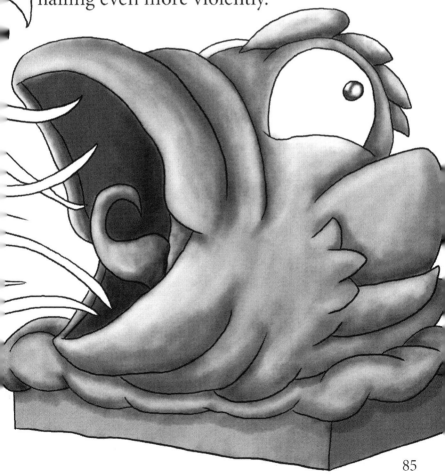

All the chirping made it hard for Squishy to think.

"If only these birds were asleep." Squishy jumped with excitement, "That's it!" In the light alert in nest, in light's absence take a rest. If I turn out the lights, the birds will fall asleep."

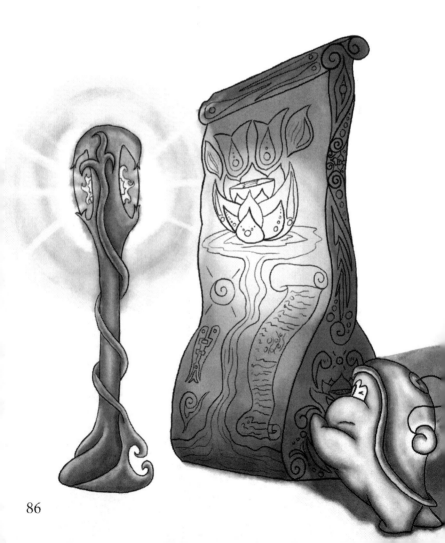

Squishy began looking for a way to turn off the rooms light when he noticed three large statues. Squishy began pushing a statue and moved it in front of the first light. The statue began to create a shadow. Once the shadow had engulfed the first baby bird, it fell asleep immediately. Squishy could freely move the next statues in front of the other bird's lights. One by one Squishy put the birds to sleep, and then made his way across the room to the next door and opened it.

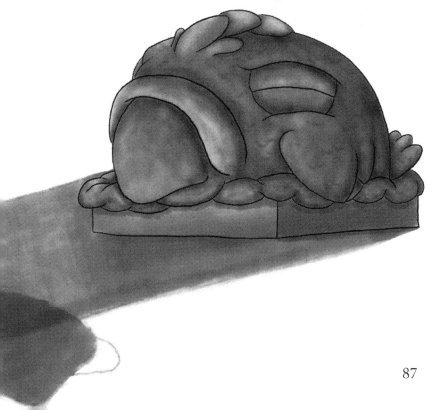

The next room was pitch black.
Squishy, just like Emily, was afraid of
the dark. So Squishy shined his light as
bright as he could. The walls began to
move. The walls were made up of panels
that looked as if insects were crawling
across them. Squishy froze in fright,
but the tiny panels on the walls stopped
moving. Squishy built up his courage and
continued walking to find the next door.
As he moved forward, the wall panels
began to move again. Frozen, Squishy
noticed the walls stopped moving when
he stopped moving. Squishy walked to
every corner of the room and found no
door leading out. Just the door he came
through. Squishy looked at his map and
read the next clue.

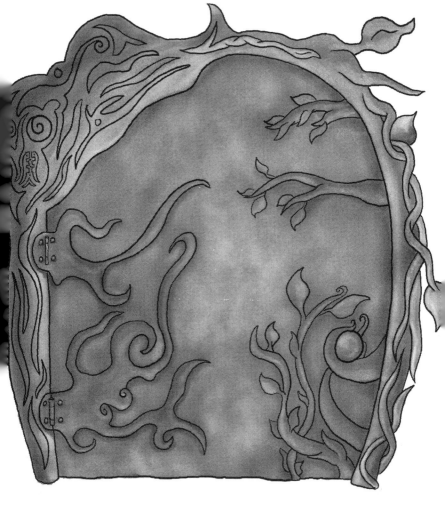

Cannot see, the path to the other side,
The exit lies, where darkness resides.

"The exit lies where darkness resides?" Squishy pondered the riddle. "I'm not afraid of anything as long as I have my light!"

Squishy was stunned with realization. He had to continue without his light. Dimming his light, Squishy could see the walls begin to change. Squishy crept across the floor, shaking with each step. Squishy was about to give up and turn his light back on when he bumped into a wall. This wall wasn't like the walls he had touched before. It was wooden, it was a door! Squishy looked for a doorknob and turned it. The door flung open, and a gust of wind hurled Squishy out of the room.

Squishy found himself outside, at the top of the Dark Shadow's Tower. Looking around, Squishy realized he was on another bridge this time with a room at the other end. Shadows and darkness seemed to flow out from the room like a waterfall.

"This is where the shadow is keeping Emily. I can feel it." Squishy, gained his second wind and ran across the bridge.

Approaching the end of the bridge Squishy noticed the strange room's door was slowly opening. The Dark Shadow's evil energy flowed out like a river let loose by a dam. Having second thoughts Squishy stopped in his tracks. "I have to save Emily. I have to go in." Squishy marched into the shadows.

12

Fear Overcome

Window light illuminates her face.

Finally found his beloved friend.

But something felt out of place

This was not going to be the end.

Emily was sitting at the far end of the room. She sat on her knees, head bowed, the last bit of moonlight shined on her through a small window. Squishy leaped towards Emily, excitement filled every

inch of his shell, but he could not move.
Something held him down. Struggling
to free himself, Squishy pulled his body
left and right, forward and backward, up
and down. But his efforts were wasted.
Looking around for a way out, he saw
what had a hold of him. A dark shadowy
force came from the shadiest corner of the
room. It spoke in a deep raspy voice.

"You have wasted your time coming
here." The dark force crept out of the
shadows.

The Dark Shadow was like a black flame and had dark glowing eyes with an evil jack-o-lantern grin.

"Emily!!" Squishy yelled. Emily looked up, her eyes cold and fearful. But when she saw Squishy, her eyes seemed to thaw and began to show the slightest glow of hope.

"You are too late," the Dark Shadow laughed wickedly. "She belongs to her fears now."

"No!" Squishy protested. "I'm here to help guide Emily through the shadows. She doesn't have to be afraid when I'm here." Squishy shined his light as bright as he could. The Dark Shadow winced at the sudden burst of light and then proceeded towards Squishy as if the light had no effect.

"HAHAHA, your light has no power here. Emily's fears provide all the power I need in order to destroy you." The Dark Shadow reached down, grabbed Squishy's light, and then proceeded to squeeze. Squishy buckled over in pain struggling to shine his light brighter.

CRACK!

Squishy's light began to break. The Dark Shadow's force was too much for Squishy's light. Squishy's light started to go out when a soft voice came from the back of the room.

"I'm not afraid of you," a voice whispered.

"What?" The Dark Shadow released Squishy and turned to see Emily standing in the moonlight, with eyes no longer frozen in fear. Her eyes were full of fire and courage.

"I'm not afraid anymore," spoke Emily with confidence. "You no longer have my fear!"

The Dark Shadow tore towards Emily laughing madly, "I will show you what real FEAR is!"

"Squishy... shine your light!" Emily yelled.

Squishy looked up and made a sudden realization. The strange voice that whispered to me at the bridge was Emily. Squishy then noticed Emily standing up to the Dark Shadow.

"Shine your light!" Emily yelled once more. With that Squishy felt a power build up inside himself like never before. Squishy's light began to glow boldly.

"What is this?" Feeling its back begin to burn, the Dark Shadow stopped. "It… It cannot be."

The Dark Shadow turned to see not just Squishy's light glowing, but Squishy himself was glowing too.

Light suddenly burst from Squishy illuminating the entire room.

"NO!" the Dark Shadow screeched. "Fear me."

"I am no longer afraid of the shadows," said Emily. "You no longer have power over me!" Emily grabbed Squishy and held him tight. Squishy's light burned brighter and the Dark Shadow dissolved into nothingness. Emily fell to her knees crying, holding Squishy. Squishy's light burned ever brighter. The Dark Shadow's Tower glowed and light shot out illuminating the night sky. Squishy opened his eyes and felt drops of water fall on his shell.

"You came for me," wept Emily. "You saved me!"

Squishy looked up and smiled, "I missed you, let's go home."

Emily continued to hold Squishy as tears of joy poured from her eyes.

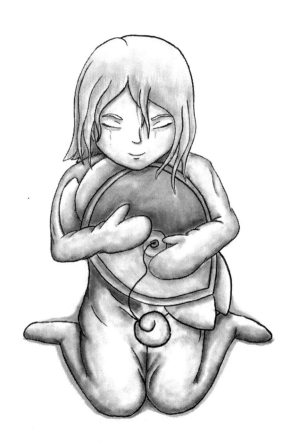

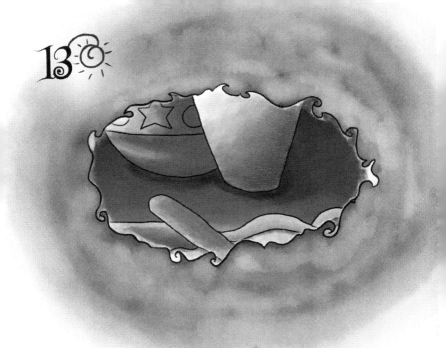

13

Home

Squishy and Emily left the Dark Tower and headed towards the Mushroom Forest. It was time to go home. Squishy looked back at the Dark Tower and noticed the gloomy cloud that once orbited the tower had been replaced with a stunning sunrise. The Tower changed as well. It no longer appeared dark and unmoving. The branches were swaying in the wind and a green hue returned to its base. The Dark Shadow's presence no longer lingered there.

Squishy led Emily back to the forest clearing where they both had originally entered this strange world. At the center of the clearing was a blue glowing ring just like before. Inside the ring Emily could see her room. Emily picked up Squishy and dashed towards the portal home.

THUMP!

Emily halted. Squishy leaped from Emily's arms shining his light as bright as he could to protect her.

"Turn that thing off boy." Bole exclaimed.

"Boletas! It's you!" Squishy said with excitement.

"Aye, of course it is! Is this the friend you were searching for?"

"I'm Emily," she said. "Squishy saved me from the Dark Shadow!"

"What!? You actually did it? You defeated the Dark Shadow!?" Bole asked surprised. "You must have been what created that great light I saw in the distance… I knew you could do it boy!" Bole leapt forward and gave Squishy a hug.

"I couldn't have done it without Emily. She truly defeated it by overcoming her fears." Squishy reminded Emily of the accomplishments she had made. Emily

blushed with pride and reached forward to shake Bole's hand.

"Nice to meet you, Bole," Emily said. "I heard how you helped Squishy find me. Thank you"

"The pleasure is all mine ma'am. Now is this the portal that you came though?"

asked Bole.

Squishy looked at Bole questioningly, "I thought you opened this portal? Who opened it?"

"I did," a soft, sweet voice came down from the sky. Madri gracefully landed in front of the three stunned adventurers. "What a beautiful girl. I am so glad you will make it home safely."

Boletas bowed before her. "Squishy kneel down. That's Madri, the Queen of the Fae."

"No need to bow Bole. He knows all too well who I am. This forest and I owe Squishy and Emily our lives, which is

105

why I have opened this portal to their home." Madri curtsied towards Squishy and Emily and directed them towards the portal. "You could stay here if you would like."

"Thank you," Emily said. "Your forest is beautiful, but we want to get home to our family."

Madri looked down sadly, "I am afraid you must go back alone, Emily."

Squishy jumped at this. "What do you mean alone? I am going too."

"Squishy, Emily has grown up and no longer fears the shadows. She has to go back alone." Madri gestured towards the portal.

"But I need her," Squishy cried out.

"This world needs your light Squishy," Madri argued. "There is still more darkness in this world your light can help fight."

Squishy latched on to Emily crying, "It was because of Emily my light was strong

enough to defeat the Dark Shadow. I cannot fight the darkness without her!"

"Squishy, it will be ok." Emily placed Squishy on the ground.

"Squishy is right however. As long as you believe in Squishy, Emily, your link to this world will not be broken." Madri rested a reassuring hand on Squishy. "When Squishy needs you most, your link will open a portal. Just as when you needed Squishy, your magic brought him to life."

"I have magic?" asked Emily.

"Yes! All creatures do in this world! But you must be getting back. I cannot hold this portal open much longer." Madri motioned towards the portal.

Emily looked at Squishy and hugged him one last time. "I will never forget you, Squishy. I will always love you." Emily then rushed to Bole and Madri and hugged them both as well. "Thank you all again for everything," Emily jumped through the glowing blue ring.

Traveling through the glowing blue ring.

Leaving fears they no longer sting.

Morning rises so flees the night.

When darkness comes so must the light.

Squishy will return

About the Author

Wes Thorpe is an Elementary Art Teacher living in Colorado Springs, Colorado. He found his passion for teaching and writing while working for a before and after school childcare program. In addition to teaching, writing and drawing; Wes enjoys yoga, reading, and playing video games.

Learn more about W. Thorpe and his books at
www.wthorpebooks.com

wathorpebooks@gmail.com

Facebook: @wthorpebooks
Instagram: @wthorpebooks

21032843R00061

Made in the USA
Lexington, KY
08 December 2018